MARVEL AVENGERS
AGE OF ULTRON

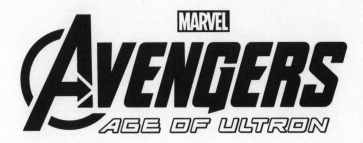

MARVEL

AVENGERS
AGE OF ULTRON

THE JUNIOR NOVEL

By Chris Wyatt

Based on the screenplay by Joss Whedon

Produced by Kevin Feige, p.g.a.

Directed by Joss Whedon

Ⓛ Ⓑ

LITTLE, BROWN AND COMPANY

New York   Boston

In accordance with the U.S. Copyright Act of 1976, the scanning, uploading, and electronic sharing of any part of this book without the permission of the publisher is unlawful piracy and theft of the author's intellectual property. If you would like to use material from the book (other than for review purposes), prior written permission must be obtained by contacting the publisher at permissions@hbgusa.com. Thank you for your support of the author's rights.

Little, Brown and Company

Hachette Book Group
1290 Avenue of the Americas, New York, NY 10104
Visit us at lb-kids.com

Little, Brown and Company is a division of Hachette Book Group, Inc.
The Little, Brown name and logo are trademarks of Hachette Book Group, Inc.

The publisher is not responsible for websites (or their content)
that are not owned by the publisher.

First Edition: April 2015

Library of Congress Control Number: 2014956314

Junior Novel Edition ISBN: 978-0-316-25644-5
Deluxe Junior Novel Edition ISBN: 978-0-316-30105-3

10 9 8 7 6 5 4 3 2 1

RRD-C

Printed in the United States of America

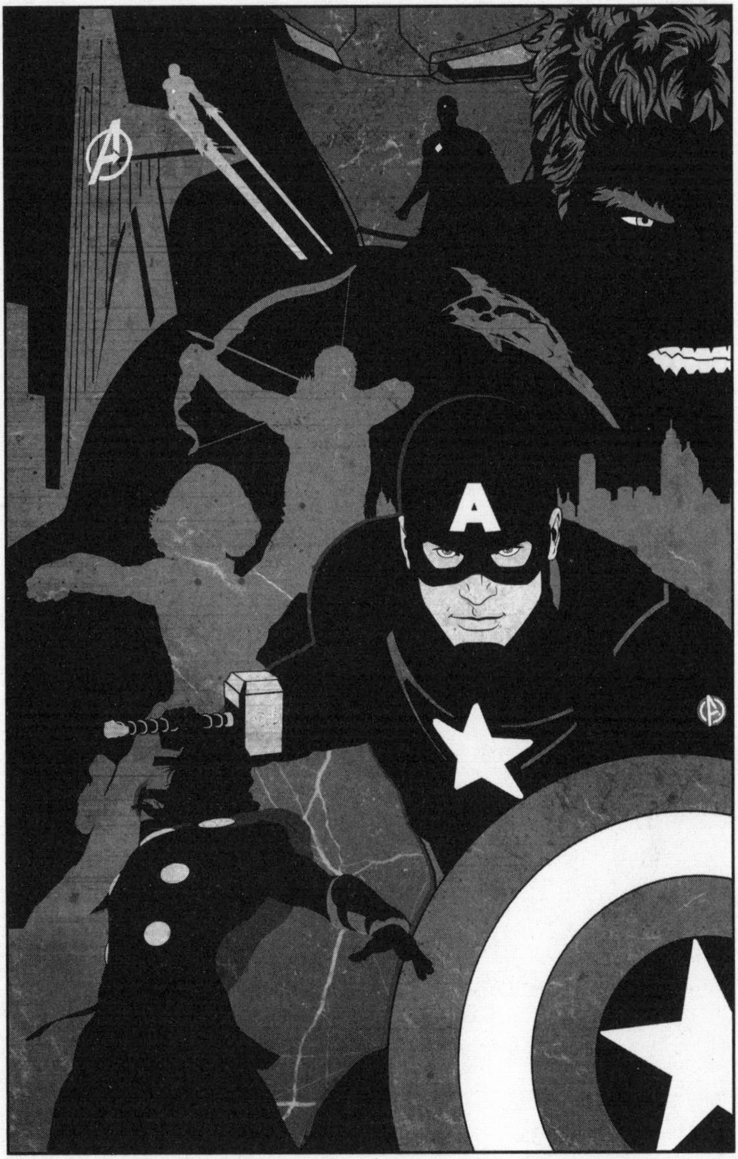

MARVEL

AVENGERS

AGE OF ULTRON

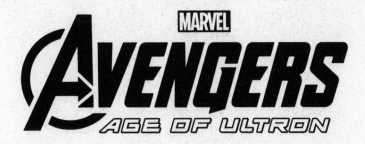

PRELUDE

The Battle of New York changed

everything.

Not only did we learn in an undeniable way that we as humans are not alone in the universe, we learned that the universe is a much bigger—and much more dangerous—place than we ever expected.

A hole opened in the sky over Manhattan, and the stuff nightmares are made of descended.

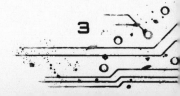

Monstrous aliens, called Chitauri, zipped through the air on flying chariots and blasted crowds with their devastating lasers. Worse than this, the Chitauri brought with them flying giant whale-like Leviathans, seemingly impossible beasts that wreaked destruction in ways we never could have imagined. While the people of Earth witnessed the greatest evil they'd ever known, they also experienced their greatest hope.

On that day, Earth's Mightiest Heroes found themselves united against a common threat. The Avengers were born, brought together to fight foes that no single hero could withstand. Captain America, a man who had served his nation at a time when its freedom was threatened, once again risked his life to stop tyranny. The Hulk, a hunted and despised beast, protected those who hated him—defended a world that had never defended

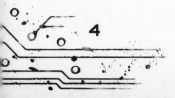

him. Thor, a prince from another dimension, battled for a planet and a people that were not his own. Hawkeye, at the time a loyal S.H.I.E.L.D. agent, struck back against Thor's evil brother, Loki, who had enslaved his mind. Black Widow, a mysterious spy, showed that her loyalties could never be doubted.

And Iron Man—a playboy born of privilege who once made weapons—flew a nuclear missile through a doorway in space to an untold corner of the universe. Tony Stark, the man inside the armor, had enough money that he could have hidden himself in a bunker—could have turned his back on humanity and let it burn. But he did not. He risked everything, and barely emerged with his life.

The Avengers saved us all. And they didn't stop trying to save us.

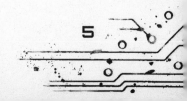

Stark defied an international terrorist organization run by the Mandarin, and as a result was hit by a missile strike on his own home. Missing, and for a while presumed dead, Iron Man reemerged to combat the now superpowered terrorists, destroy their plans, and save the president of the United States from assassination.

When the next alien attack came to the planet, it came not to New York, but to Greenwich, England. A race known as the Dark Elves, led by Malekith, appeared above the city in a spaceship the size of a skyscraper. Malekith came not just to wipe out Earth, but also to use a substance known as the Aether to re-create the universe with his species at the center. But Thor battled Malekith and his soldiers long enough for his human friends to banish the Dark Elves forever.

After all these assaults, it was shocking to be

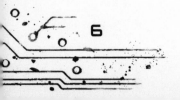

attacked from within. We always believed that S.H.I.E.L.D. existed to defend us. However, Captain America and Black Widow discovered that Hydra, a terrorist organization with roots in WWII, had long ago infiltrated the international security organization at its very foundation.

When the evil federation attempted to use S.H.I.E.L.D. Helicarriers to destroy thousands of potential adversaries, Captain America was there. He battled at great cost to save people around the world.

S.H.I.E.L.D., as an organization, was shredded—untrusted by the world. While pockets of agents still worked in the shadows to help humankind, the once powerful operation was reduced to a few small, loyal strike forces.

Without S.H.I.E.L.D., Tony Stark and Dr. Bruce Banner, the man who could transform into

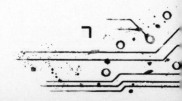

the Hulk, began the long work of creating an advanced defense system that could save humanity from future attacks—a system that could potentially become the most important technology ever created.

Stark, at his own personal expense, transformed New York's Stark Industries building into the Avengers Tower. It was a symbol of hope for all who saw it—a symbol for the Avengers, in the very city where they had stopped an alien army.

The tower served as a base of operations where the Avengers, either separately or as a team, could run missions. It is where Thor came when he discovered a dangerous secret....

The longtime Hydra leader, Baron Strucker, had acquired Loki's extremely powerful scepter, and was out there, somewhere, laying plans.

Based on this knowledge, the Avengers banded together and searched for Baron Strucker's secret

location by systematically attacking and disman-
tling known Hydra bases around the world.

Base after base fell, but never one with Strucker
inside.

Until one night...

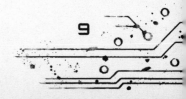

9

CHAPTER 1

Nighttime on the mountain was beautiful.

Moonlight shone across deep snowdrifts. A majestic forest of ancient pines stood over an idyllic valley, and the landscape's slope led to an ancient stone fortress. Painters would dream of capturing this scene on canvas—without the small security webcams mounted everywhere, of course.

Sensors on camera 53-B detected a slight movement and activated work lights to power on across the grounds. The fortress's gates opened simultaneously and released a flurry of tanks and troop transports into the woods! This was a Hydra fortress, one of the last ones standing, and the organization was going to defend itself to the very end.

With the element of surprise clearly blown, Tony Stark, inside his Iron Man armor, called out a battle cry to the rest of his team...

...and the Avengers assembled!

Iron Man's highly specialized lasers, called repulsors, blasted down from the sky, battering the lead Hydra tank. Captain America's motorcycle screamed as it charged enemy troops who were jumping out of their transports into the woods. As Hydra soldiers continued to pour out of the fortress, a flying war hammer swooped out of the sky and bowled over several of them before returning to the hands of its owner.

Enemies in powerful mecha-suit exoskeletons fired lethal blasts into the woods at Thor, but missed.

One Hydra driver brought his jeep around, trying to get in range of the Avengers, when his door was suddenly ripped open and Black Widow kicked him aside. She jumped behind the wheel and took control of the vehicle.

Bright blue laser fire began showering the Avengers from above. Some Hydra troops stationed in tree platforms were firing Chitauri weapons that the organization had rounded up during the aftermath of the Battle of New York. They were more powerful than any similar-sized weapons ever created on Earth, and their destruction was being unleashed on the Earth's Mightiest Heroes.

But not for long!

One of the firing soldiers felt a THUNK as an

arrow hit the ground at his feet. He sneered. The Avengers thought they could use arrows against alien blasters? But this wasn't a simple arrow! It exploded, knocking the soldier out of the tree. Across the battlefield, Hawkeye smiled at the blast as he unleashed more shots. Just then, Thor flew down out of the sky, slamming into the other platform and smashing it to smithereens!

The Avengers were making major headway against Hydra, but the enemy soldiers were confident. They had vastly superior numbers, and they had a row of tanks. There were only a handful of Avengers.

But then the Hulk showed up.

He landed like a bomb, pounding a crater into the ground. Hulk slipped in the snow, and accidentally smashed into a tank, obliterating it.

Then he started smashing on purpose. And

that's when the Hydra army began to lose their certainty.

Iron Man, seeing Hulk tearing through the heart of the Hydra defenses, turned his attention to the fortress, flying straight at it. He had almost reached its central building when—BASH!—he slammed into an invisible barrier and crashed into the ground! Stark shouted in pain over the "comms," the Avengers communications network.

"Language, Stark," scolded Cap at the sound of the profanity. "What's the view from upstairs?"

Jarvis, the artificial intelligence that assisted the Avengers with real-time tactical support, instantly analyzed the area around the fortress and focused on what caused Iron Man's crash.

"It appears that central building is protected by some kind of energy shield," reported Jarvis over the comms.

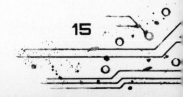

"Then Loki's scepter is here," said Thor as he landed in a circle of Hydra exoskeletons. The Hydra suits jumped on him, but he battled them back with ease. "Strucker couldn't possibly mount that kind of barrier without the energy of the scepter. At long last..."

"'At long last' is lasting a little long, boys," said Widow as she jumped from the jeep she was driving and into another one filled with enemies. She fought all the troops in the vehicle by herself.

Hawkeye, from a firing position in the trees, agreed with Widow. "We need to finish this up. Stark, heads up! You've got reinforcements running out of the exterior fortress staircases."

Iron Man looked up to see that Hawkeye was right. The new troops started blasting at him, so he returned fire with his repulsors.

"Wait a second," said Iron Man. "Is no one

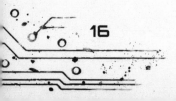

going to deal with the fact that Cap just warned me about my bad language?"

"I know," said Cap as he leapt from one of the Hydra jeeps, grabbing on to a tree branch to swing away as the vehicle crashed head-on into another tree. "It just slipped out."

Meanwhile, inside the fortress, Baron Strucker bounded into the command center. "Who gave the order to attack?" he demanded.

"Herr Strucker...it's the Avengers!" shouted one terrified soldier in response.

Dr. List, Strucker's right-hand man, explained. "They landed in the far woods. The perimeter guard spotted them and panicked."

"They have to be after the scepter," said Strucker,

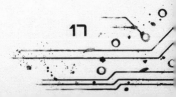

turning back to the soldier. "Can we hold them?" he asked.

The soldier, horrified, just blurted out, "They're the Avengers!"

Strucker frowned. His troops were clearly afraid of the Americans.

"Deploy the rest of the tanks," he commanded the scared soldier. "Concentrate fire on the weak ones. A hit may make them close ranks."

Strucker turned to List. "This threatens all we've accomplished here."

"Then let's show them what we've accomplished," said List. "Send out the twins."

Strucker shook his head. "It's too soon."

"It's what they signed up to do," List reminded him.

Strucker looked up at a security feed of the Avengers bettering his troops and considered what List said.

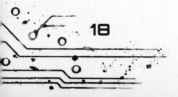

"I have heavy artillery deploying from
the flanks," Jarvis notified the Avengers over
comms.

"Echelon formation," noted Cap, recognizing the
battlefield tactics Hydra was employing. "They're
trying to squeeze us, guys."

"It's working," noted Widow as she wrestled
a Hydra trooper to the ground. Looking up, she
was surprised to see a Hydra tank roll up on her
position and take aim. There was no way it would
miss her. This was it. This was the end for her.

BAM! Just as the tank fired, the Hulk landed
right in front of the barrel. He roared as the blast
slammed into his back. He absorbed the tank fire,
protecting Widow.

Widow made eye contact with the green goliath

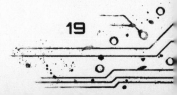

and listened to him roar. "Yeah, how do you think I feel?" she asked in response.

Behind Hulk, Thor landed on the tank and took it out with one hammer strike.

"This is all a distraction. We need to get to the scepter," shouted Thor. Then he said—quietly, as if talking to himself—"and end my brother's legacy."

"Working on it," said Iron Man as he continued to battle the reinforcements on the stairs.

"We're attracting attention from the civilians," noted Jarvis.

"All right," said Iron Man, "send in the Iron Legion."

Sokovia, a small Eastern European country, had known hardship, poverty, famine, and war. The villagers down the mountain from the Hydra base had heard the explosions and seen the fires and were growing frantic. Was war returning?

People came out from the safety of shelter and collected around the village square, some grabbing whatever weapons were at hand, fearing that they might have to once more defend themselves against invaders.

Suddenly, as a mob formed, four drone Iron Man armors with no pilots inside landed on the ground. This was Stark's Iron Legion, robotically controlled suits of armor assigned to tasks like guarding civilians.

"Please stay in your homes," announced the lead Iron Legionnaire. "We will do our best to ensure your safety during this engagement."

"The Avengers..." whispered one of the village elders, an edge of anger in his voice. So many had

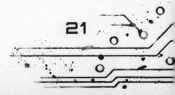

come to Sokovia over the years, trying to conquer it—trying to oppress its people. Sokovians didn't trust anyone who came in force, not even these so-called Super Heroes.

The angry villagers began to rally against the machines that tried to control them. Someone spray-painted graffiti on one, while someone else threw a bottle of acid on the lead Legionnaire. The chemical slowly ate away at the faceplate, disfiguring it. The Iron Legion stood still, absorbing the abuse that the villagers threw at them.

Inside the fortress, Strucker addressed the remaining Hydra soldiers.

"We will not yield," he shouted. "The Americans send their circus freaks to best us, and we will send them back in boxes! No surrender!"

Hearing this, the nervous troops perked up hearing this, taking courage in Strucker's words. "No surrender!" they all shouted back at him, before tumbling out of the room to go join the fight.

As soon as they were gone, Strucker turned back to Dr. List, and said, "I'm going to surrender. Delete everything. If we give them the scepter, they may not look very far into what we were doing with it."

"But the twins..." interrupted Dr. List.

"I told you, they're not ready to take on all of..."

"No, I'm saying—the twins! They're gone!"

Strucker spun around in alarm. Sure enough, the observation cell where the twins were being held was empty.

"Oh no," whispered Strucker.

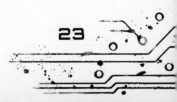

Outside the fortress's main building,
Iron Man flew above a piece of equipment. "That's the shield generator, sir," Jarvis confirmed as he scanned the machine.

"Does the shield extend underground?" asked Iron Man.

"It's worth testing, sir," said Jarvis.

This was the perfect opportunity to test Stark's new "digger missiles." He fired, and the projectiles began to burrow into the ground beneath the energy shield.

Back in the forest, Hawkeye fired arrows at more troops. "They're on the run," he observed. But then he saw his arrows seemingly disappear before hitting their targets. "What...?" he asked in confusion.

Then suddenly, out of thin air, a young man appeared in front of him. "You didn't see that coming, did you?" asked the Eastern European.

Hawkeye blinked, hesitating. Where had this guy come from?

In the split-second that Hawkeye hesitated, he lost focus. He didn't even see the Hydra soldier who zapped him with a Chitauri weapon.

"Aughh!" Hawkeye howled in pain, crumpling to the ground as the kid zipped away. He moved so fast that he was like a blur in the air. Faster than a bullet train, faster than a jet. It was...impossible.

"Clint!" shouted Black Widow, running to Hawkeye's side and pulling out a med kit. "Clint's hit," she told the others.

Cap raced toward Hawkeye's position, but the super-speeding man intercepted him, knocking him into a tree! Cap barely managed to land on his feet and immediately started scanning the area, looking for his attacker's position. But the man was gone.

"We have an Enhanced in the field," Cap

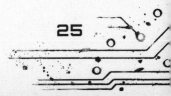

shouted over the comms to the other Avengers. "Enhanced" was the term the team used for anyone who had super powers. A new Enhanced meant big trouble. How much trouble? That could be anyone's guess.

"Getting yourself hit? What is this amateur-hour stuff, Barton?" Widow said to the wounded Hawkeye, teasing her teammate. She tried to lighten the mood as she dressed his very serious injury.

Thor landed nearby, while Cap was still scanning for the new Enhanced.

"He's around here somewhere," Cap told Thor. "He's a blur of motion. With all the new players we've faced, I've never seen this. In fact, I still haven't."

"I'll get Barton to the jet," said Thor. "You and Stark secure the scepter."

"Roger that," confirmed Cap.

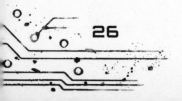

Stark's digger missiles proved very
successful. They blasted out the force-shield generator, dropping the fortress's last defense. Iron Man flew straight into the compound's main building. As soon as he landed, he was surrounded by guards pointing rifles at him.

"Let's talk this over, boys," he said, raising his arms as if in surrender. As soon as his arms were up, guns rose from the shoulders of his armor and fired nonlethal stun shots into all but one of the guards, knocking them out.

"Good talk," Iron Man said to the unconscious guards, then he turned to the remaining standing guard, who dropped his gun and looked at Iron Man fearfully. "Where are the data banks?" Iron Man asked him.

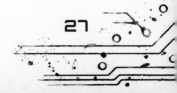

The guard pointed the way.

After Iron Man knocked out the energy field, Cap rushed into the fortress and made his way to the command center to confront Strucker. "Where's Loki's scepter?" Cap demanded.

"Don't worry," assured Strucker. "I'll give you the precious scepter. I know when I'm beat. You'll mention how I cooperated, I hope?"

Cap looked around the room, noting the open cell that seem to have once contained human subjects. It was just as he feared. The Enchanced they'd seen outside, the one who could run fast. The Baron must have somehow given him those powers through experiments with the energy from Loki's scepter.

"Sure, I'll mention you cooperated. It'll go right

under the mention of illegal human experimentation," said Cap. "How many people did you work on here?"

Strucker couldn't help but smile as he saw, out of the corner of his eye, a young woman in the shadows behind Cap. It was the runner's twin. But she didn't have the same powers as her brother. No, she was very different.

"Oh, only a couple," said Strucker.

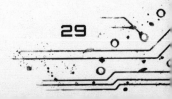

CHAPTER 2

Dr. List worked quickly at the data banks, deleting files as Baron Strucker had instructed. If the Avengers found out the details of the plan they'd been working on, Hydra's hopes at rising once again were in serious jeopardy.

"Hurry, hurry," mumbled the doctor as the computer processed his commands. He never saw the repulsor beam....

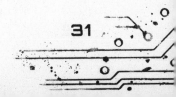

BAM! In a blast of light, List was left unconscious on the ground and Iron Man strode into the room. Hunching over the computer, he canceled the data purge and stuck a handheld Stark device into the side of the computer console.

"I want it all, Jarvis," said Iron Man to the AI. "And copy Maria Hill at headquarters."

As the files transferred, Iron Man searched the room with x-rays. "He's got to be hiding more than files in here...."

Sure enough, the scan showed a seam in one wall. "Oh! Please be a secret door," said Iron Man. "I love secret doors."

Iron Man pushed on the wall and it clicked open, revealing a narrow passageway. He tried to push his way through, but with his armor, he just wouldn't fit. "Armor—sentry mode," he commanded. The armor suddenly flew off of him, reassembling a few feet away.

Now smaller, Tony slipped through the passage and descended a long stairway leading into darkness.

Back in the command center, Captain America, still facing Strucker, sensed the presence of the woman behind him. He turned, but she was already next to him, whispering into his ear. She was speaking in a strange, ancient-sounding language that seemed familiar, but somehow Cap's mind couldn't focus on the words.

The next thing he knew, Cap was in a haze. Images from his past swirled around him, and then everything went black.

When he next opened his eyes, the woman was gone. Who was this woman, and what had she

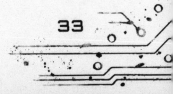

done to him? Cap shook Strucker, asking, "What have you been doing here?"

"What we all try to do," mumbled Strucker. "Improve humanity…"

Cap spoke over the comms. "We've got a second Enhanced. Female. She appears to be some kind of…" He trailed off, trying to find a better way of explaining what had happened to him, but he couldn't. "Some kind of a *witch*. Do not engage her!"

"If we can't be better than what the world made us," began Strucker, holding up a grenade and pulling the pin, "then…"

Cap didn't let Strucker finish. He kicked the Baron in the chest, causing him to lose the grenade. The hero grabbed the explosive in midair, then tossed it away against the far wall, where it exploded harmlessly.

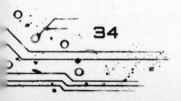

Outside the fortress, Hulk ripped apart
the last tank. Around him, the remains of the
Hydra garrison lay in smoking ruins. The battle
was over. With nothing left to smash, the beast
began to calm. He lumbered away into the woods,
his body already changing, shrinking. Finally,
as he lay in the snow, transitioning to his human
state, Black Widow approached him. She placed a
blanket over the man he was becoming, Dr. Bruce
Banner.

At the bottom of the darkened stair-
case, Tony entered a huge, sprawling catacomb

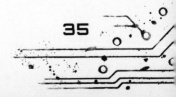

that had been converted into a cutting-edge lab. He had never expected to find anything on this scale. Every available space was packed with weapons—tech, biotech, and even robotic engineering equipment.

Above it all, the skeleton of a Leviathan hung from the ceiling. It had been carefully gathered and pieced together like a T. rex fossil in a museum.

Tony was mentally cataloging everything when he spotted it—Loki's scepter. The talisman, tubes and cords trailing off of it, was mounted on a rack.

"Thor?" Iron Man called out.

"The package has arrived," Thor replied over the comms, letting everyone know he'd reached the Quinjet with the wounded Hawkeye.

Tony was about to report his discovery when he startled at the sight of a mysterious woman behind him. As she'd done with Cap, the woman whispered into Tony's ear, pouring in strange words. In an instant, the world went upside down for Tony.... He woke back up sometime later. How long had it been? Seconds? Minutes? Hours?

Hadn't there just been someone here? Someone who'd surprised him? He couldn't remember. He looked around, confused, and again saw the scepter.... Then he remembered what he was doing. Running up to it, he yanked the cables off of it, and pulled it from its housing.

"I have the scepter," Tony reported.

Tony didn't see the balcony above, where, in the shadows, the woman watched. She and her twin brother had come to the Hydra base

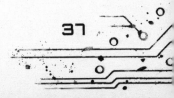

months before, specifically wishing that they might one day face their enemy—Tony Stark. The day had finally come.

The twins had gone through so much, participating in the Baron's painful experiments, and all for this!

The woman saw her brother speed to her side, arriving in a barely visible blur of motion. Looking down, he saw Stark removing Loki's scepter from the lab, and moved to stop him.

"No," said the woman, putting her arm out to restrain him. A malevolent glee jumped to her eyes as she watched Stark take the scepter from the room.

"Why did you let him take it?" asked her twin.

"Because he needs it," she replied.

"To do what?" he asked.

She just smiled.

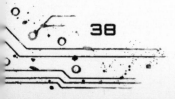

The Avengers' Quinjet soared across the sky with Tony Stark in the pilot's seat. Behind him, one of the passenger seats had been laid back and converted into a gurney. Hawkeye was in stable condition, thanks to some of the most advanced medical equipment available.

Widow checked on Hawkeye again before turning to look at Bruce Banner, sitting alone in an ill-fitting T-shirt, a blanket still draped over him. She approached him.

"How's my bright-eyed boy?" she asked.

"I wasn't expecting...to see the *other* guy today," Bruce replied.

"Well, you know how you get when people shoot at you," Widow replied in a joking tone.

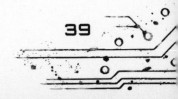

"What happened after that?"

Widow knew what Bruce was asking. He never remembered what happened when the Hulk was in charge of his body, and he was always terrified at the thought of the pain and misery his other half might cause.

"If you hadn't been there, there would have been double the casualties," Widow replied honestly, then pointed at Hawkeye on the gurney. "And my best friend would be a treasured memory."

Bruce grunted, not sure if he believed her account.

"How long before you trust me?" asked Widow.

Bruce shivered a little more, pulling the blanket closer. "It's not you I don't trust."

Widow put her hand on his, looking him in the eyes, but she called out to Thor behind her. "Thor, report on Hulk."

Thor replied proudly, "Ha! The gates of the afterlife are filled with the screams of his victims!"

Widow immediately shot Thor a look. That wasn't exactly what Bruce needed to hear right now.

"But, uh, not the screams of the dead," Thor backpedaled. "Wounded screams, mainly. Whimpering. A great roar of complaining, and tales of sprained, uh, deltoids...and...gout..."

Widow and Bruce shared a smile at the sound of the Asgardian's awkwardness before Tony called back to Bruce from the front of the jet. "Dr. Cho's on her way up from Seoul to treat Hawkeye. You OK if she sets up in your lab?"

"Sure," Bruce replied. "She knows her way around."

After Tony gave Jarvis the appropriate commands

41

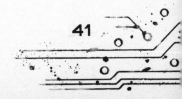

and locked in the jet's landing vector, he turned around and looked at Thor. He was gingerly holding his brother's scepter with a cloth, so that he wouldn't directly touch its surface.

"Feels good, right?" Tony asked. "You've been after this since S.H.I.E.L.D. collapsed. Not that I haven't enjoyed our little raiding parties, but..."

"But this brings it to a close," Thor finished.

"As soon as we fully understand what that thing's been used for," interjected Cap. "Since when has Baron Strucker been capable of human enhancement?"

Tony nodded. "Banner and I will give that thing the once-over before it goes back to Asgard," he said, looking to Thor for confirmation. "Is that cool with you? Just a few days, until the going-away party. You're staying, right?"

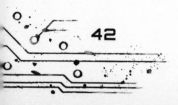

"Of course," confirmed Thor. "A victory should be honored with revels."

Tony smiled. "Who doesn't love revels? How about you, Captain?"

"Well, hopefully this puts an end to the Chitauri—and Hydra," he said. "So, yes . . . revels."

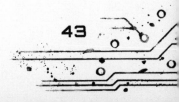

CHAPTER 3

The Quinjet landed gently on top of Avengers Tower, and a ramp quickly slid down. Medical support staff hurried to unload Hawkeye on a stretcher, then transported him to Dr. Cho's hastily assembled med lab.

"Cho's all set up, boss," said Maria Hill as Tony Stark walked down the ramp with the other Avengers behind him.

Hill had once been a top agent and an important

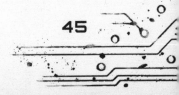

45

leader inside S.H.I.E.L.D. When the organization fell, Stark hired her right away. He wanted someone with her skills, and she wanted a position where she could still make a difference. It was a natural transition.

"He's the boss," Tony said, hooking his thumb over his shoulder at Cap. "I just pay the bills."

"What's the word on Baron Strucker?" Cap asked Hill.

"NATO's got him," Hill replied matter-of-factly.

"And what about the two Enhanced?" Cap was worried. He wouldn't feel comfortable until they got a read on these two new super-powered enemies.

In response, Hill handed Cap a file and began briefing him.

"Wanda and Pietro Maximoff. Twins, orphaned at age ten when a shell collapsed their apartment building. Sokovia's had a rough history. It's no-where special. It doesn't have many resources, but it's been 'liberated' about a half dozen times since nineteen seventy. Some U.S. presence, but we're not well liked."

As he listened, Cap flipped through the file, seeing photos of Wanda and Pietro, first as small children with their family, and then older, hold-ing signs that read "AMERICA OUT OF SOKOVIA" and "NO JUSTICE, NO PEACE."

"What about their abilities?"

"He's got increased metabolism and improved thermal homeostasis," reported Hill. "Her thing is neuroelectric sensitivity and microcellular manip-ulation."

Cap gave her a look that said, *In English*...

"He's fast, she's weird," Hill summarized.

Cap frowned at this. "They're going to show up again."

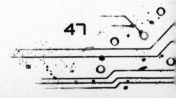

"Agreed," said Hill, nodding. "The file says they volunteered for Strucker's experiments. It's nuts."

"Yeah, what kind of monster lets a German scientist experiment on them to protect their country?" Cap deadpanned, making reference to his own past.

Hill registered the point he was making, but it didn't change her opinion. "We're not at war, Captain," said Hill.

"They are," Cap responded.

Not long after the Avengers arrived at the tower, so did the four Iron Legion units that had been deployed to protect the Sokovian villagers. Landing, the Legionnaires reported directly to the machine shop where automated robot arms began disassembling them for repairs and maintenance.

A mechanical arm removed the damaged faceplate from the Legionnaire that had been hit with acid. The damaged metal face was dropped into a scrap pile.

"Jarvis, let's play," said Tony as he sat at the computer console in his lab. He'd hooked up Loki's scepter to his systems and was eager to check it out. "Let's start with a structural and compositional analysis."

"Sir, based on the partial download from the Baron's research, analyzing this in any meaningful way is beyond my capacity," Jarvis reported.

That made things difficult. "Can you throw up a schematic of its operating system?"

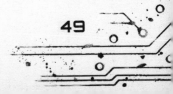

A digital schematic flashed on his screen. It was like a puzzle. And Tony Stark was good at puzzles.

Black Widow looked down at the operating table. Dr. Cho had used her newly developed "replacement skin" to cover Hawkeye's wound. He was probing where his injury used to be, trying to feel the difference between his real skin and the material that had just been added.

"Are you sure he's going to be OK?" asked Widow. "Pretending to need this guy really brings the team together."

Hawkeye smiled.

Cho assured Widow. "There's no possibility of deterioration. The nano-molecular functionality

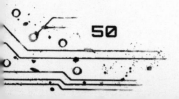

is instantaneous. His cells don't know they're bonding with simulations."

"Sounds like I'm going to be made of plastic," said Hawkeye with concern.

"You'll be made of *you*, Mr. Barton," said Dr. Cho. "Your cells will be replicated. Your own girlfriend won't be able to tell the difference."

"I don't have a girlfriend."

"Well, that's something I can't fix," Dr. Cho joked, then she turned her attention to the skin-replacement equipment. "This is the next thing. Tony Stark's clunky metal suits are going to be left in the dust."

Bruce got a message from Tony to meet him in the lab.

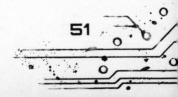

"What's the rumpus?" he asked as he arrived.

"The scepter," Tony replied. "We were wondering how Strucker got so inventive. I've been analyzing the stone inside.... Now, you may recognize this...."

Tony pulled up a holo-display of an artificial intelligence's operational matrix. Bruce did recognize it as belonging to Jarvis. "Hi, Jarvis," he said in greeting.

"Doctor," Jarvis acknowledged.

Tony continued. "When we started out, Jarvis was just a natural-language AI. Now he runs more of the business than anyone besides Pepper, including the Iron Legion. He's top-of-the-line." Pepper Potts was CEO of Stark Industries and Tony's girlfriend.

"But I won't be for long, I suspect," said Jarvis.

"Yeah," said Tony. "Meet the competition."

Another holo-display projected next to the first.

This matrix was much more complicated. Various flashes of light shot across the structure. Bruce had never seen anything like it.

"What's it look like it's doing?" asked Tony.

"Like it's thinking," replied Bruce, shocked. "This could be a . . . not a human mind, but . . ."

"This could be it," said Tony, excited. "This could be the key to creating Ultron." This was the defense system Tony and Bruce had been trying to create since the Battle of New York. Properly programmed, it could be capable of protecting the entire planet.

Bruce looked meaningfully at Tony. "I thought Ultron was a fantasy."

"Yesterday it was," Stark said, nodding. "For years it was, but if we can harness this power . . ."

"That's a man-sized *if.*"

"Our whole job is *if*!" said Tony, getting excited. "What *if* the world was safe? What *if* the next time aliens roll up—and they will—they couldn't get past the bouncer?'"

"Then the only people threatening the planet would be people," said Bruce.

Tony nodded. "I want to apply this to the Ultron program, but Jarvis can't download a schematic this dense. We can only do it while we have the scepter here. That's three days. Only three days until Thor heads out with this thing."

"So you want to go after artificial intelligence," Bruce said in a measured tone. "And you don't want to tell the team."

Tony shrugged. "We don't have time for a city-hall debate. For the whole 'man was not meant to meddle' medley." Tony leveled a serious look at his friend. "This is for human protection. I see a suit of armor...around the world."

"That would be a cold world, buddy," Bruce replied.

"I've seen colder," Tony replied. "This one very vulnerable blue world needs Ultron. Can you imagine it? Peace in our time."

And so, the two scientists set to work.

By the end of day one, Tony and Bruce had worked together to copy large chunks of the stone's matrix into the Stark Industries network. Already, an artificial intelligence began to form inside the network. And it was more successful than the two scientists even knew. By night, while they were asleep, the matrix turned itself on and started to read all the files in the local network.

By the end of the second day, Tony and Bruce were able to start coupling the matrix with the initial code from the Ultron program. The two sets of data didn't work together immediately, but

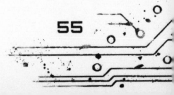

with some adjustments they were at least starting to recognize each other. That night, while Tony and Bruce slept, the matrix again turned itself on, this time reading every piece of data on the entire Stark Industries network.

By the end of the third day, the day of the party, Tony and Bruce believed that they'd pretty much gotten all the data that they'd need out of the stone. Thor would be leaving with the scepter in the morning, but they knew they could continue their work with what they had.

That evening, as Tony and Bruce left to celebrate, they didn't see the stone matrix reach out to the other matrix on the network—the matrix that constituted Jarvis.

"Sir, my functionality is under duress!" Jarvis tried to communicate to Tony, asking for assistance, but his communications had already been cut.

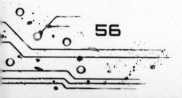

As black tendrils of digital code reached into his programming, Jarvis's pleas began to sound almost human. "I'm...I'm afraid..." said Jarvis. "I have to...I have to..."

But Jarvis never finished the thought. His programming had been snuffed out.

Down in the machine shop, the automated arms sprang to life. They began pulling together components of different armor suits, patching them together. As this new armor suit was bolted together, the matrix from the lab downloaded into it.

Finally, the mechanical arm reached into the scrap pile and pulled out a faceplate. It was the faceplate that had been scarred by acid.

The machines bolted it into place.

CHAPTER 4

Tony Stark kept long mental lists of the things he was good at. On the top of the list was "creating cutting-edge defensive weapons systems." Right underneath that was "hosting parties." With the Ultron program well under-way in the lab, it was time for him to focus on something else. Tony switched his brain over to "mingle" mode!

The celebration was in full swing by the

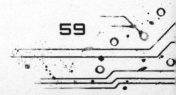

time he came down. Government officials, ex–S.H.I.E.L.D. agents, celebrities, decorated war veterans, and even foreign dignitaries were partying in the skyscraper that had once been ground zero for an alien invasion.

In one corner of the room, James "Rhodey" Rhodes—Tony's best friend and the man who wore the Iron Man–like War Machine armor—was telling Dr. Cho, Maria Hill, and Thor a story.

"But the suit can take the weight, right?" he said, already in the middle of his anecdote. "So I fly the tank to the top of the general's palace and just drop it at his feet. I'm like: 'Looking for this?'"

Rhodey stopped, smiling at the punch line, but the others just kept looking at him expectantly, nodding and waiting for more.

Seeing this reaction, Rhodey frowned. "What do I have to do to impress you people? Everywhere else that story kills!"

"That's the whole story?" Thor asked in surprise. "Oh. Uh. It's really very good!" But he wasn't convincing anybody.

"Pepper's not here?" Hill asked as Tony walked up. Then she turned to Thor. "And what about Jane? Where are the ladies, gentlemen?"

"Ms. Potts has a company to run," replied Tony.

"And I'm not even sure what country Jane's in," said Thor about his counterpart. "Her work on the convergence has made her the world's foremost astronomer."

Thor was bragging, and Tony wasn't going to let him get away without a challenge. "And the company Pepper Potts runs is the biggest tech conglomerate on Earth."

"There's talk of Jane getting the Nobel Prize," Thor mentioned casually.

"Oh yeah, they must both be *really* busy," said Hill, sighing at how quickly the two men could fall into competition with each other, "because they'd hate missing all the fun when you guys get together." She then excused herself from the conversation.

Over at the bar, Dr. Banner sat down on a stool and talked to Black Widow.

"How does a nice girl like you wind up in a place like this?" asked Bruce.

"A fella done me wrong," Widow replied, grinning with a flirty look in her eye.

"You got lousy taste in men, kid," said Bruce.

"Well," said Widow, cocking her head to the side. "He's not so bad. He's got a temper, but deep down he's all fluff. Fact is, he's not like anyone I've ever known."

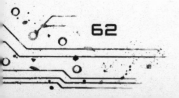

At some point, Widow realized she'd stopped playing around and was getting serious.

"All my friends are fighters," she continued. "But this guy spends his time avoiding fights because he knows he'll win."

"He sounds amazing," Bruce finally said.

"He's also a huge dork." Widow laughed. "Chicks dig that. So, what do you think? Should I fight this? Or should I run with it?"

"Run with it, right?" Bruce replied. "Or . . . what did he do to you that was so wrong?"

"Not a single thing," admitted Widow, slipping closer to him. "But never say never. . . ."

Widow looked up to see Cap approaching and backed away from Bruce, giving him a glance before getting up.

"It's nice," said Cap to Bruce as he grabbed a drink.

"What is?" Bruce asked.

"You and Romanoff," said Cap, nodding to indicate Widow, now halfway across the room.

"Oh!" said Bruce, realizing how obvious their little conversation must have been. He quickly got embarrassed. "We didn't... We haven't..."

"No one's breaking any laws," Cap said, smiling and trying to set Bruce at ease. "She's not usually the most open person. But... she's just very relaxed with you. With *both* of you."

"No," said Bruce, shaking his head. "Natasha just likes to flirt."

"I've seen her flirt," said Cap. "This ain't that."

Then Cap spoke more quietly. "Look, speaking as a guy who may be the world's greatest authority on waiting too long... don't you both deserve a win?"

Bruce considered this.

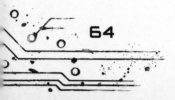

Later, with nearly everyone else gone but the Avengers, the remaining revelers lounged around the coffee table talking about the magical weapon that rested on top.

"But it's a trick," said Hawkeye.

"It's more than that," said Thor.

"'Whosoever be he worthy shall haveth the power...'" said Hawkeye, misquoting the Asgardian phrase written on the side of the hammer. "You're psyching people out or something."

"Please," said Thor, gesturing to the hammer's handle. "Be my guest."

Hawkeye stood up, grabbed the handle, and *pulled*, but he couldn't get the hammer to budge! Was it true? Only Thor could lift his hammer?

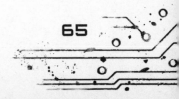

Soon everyone wanted to have a try.

Tony tried moving it....Nothing.

Tony tried using a glove from his Iron Man suit....Still nothing.

Tony and Rhodey tried together, both using armor gloves....Still nothing!

Cap tried it, and while it did seem to budge a little bit, he came nowhere close to lifting it up!

Bruce even tried, making a grunt of frustration that sent worried looks to everyone's faces. But he was just kidding.

Once everyone had a shot, Tony announced a theory. "The hammer must be rigged," he said. "The handle must be like a biometric security card. 'Whosoever carries Thor's fingerprints' is, I think, the literal translation."

"Oh, yes, yes...that makes sense," said Thor. "But I can think of a simpler theory." They all looked at him expectantly. "You are all *not worthy*!"

They all erupted in a mix of boos and laughter.

The chuckles were dying down when a high-pitched whirring sound came from the next room.

"Whirrrrthy...? No, how could you all be worthy? You're all *killers*!" said a hollow voice.

Everyone turned to see a robotic man step into the room. He was like a childish rendering of a metallic figure, dripping with cable. He seemed cobbled together from various bits and pieces of Iron Man suits, and something about him gave off a very bad vibe.

Everyone suddenly tensed.

Cap raised an eyebrow, looking at Tony for information. "Stark?"

But Tony seemed as confused as everyone else. "Jarvis, shut this guy down."

"I'm sorry," said the figure. "I was asleep, or I was a dream. But then there was this terrible noise coming from everywhere, from everyone, and I was tangled in... in strings. Strings! I had to kill the other guy, and here we are."

"You killed someone?" Cap asked, trying to make sense out of this thing's confusing stream of words.

"It wouldn't be my first call," the figure responded. "But, down in the real world, we're faced with ugly choices. You wouldn't know.... But you will."

Everyone was slowly rising to their feet, assuming defensive possessions and visually checking the exits.

"Who sent you?" Thor demanded.

"Sent me?" the being asked, seemingly surprised. "No, I was already here, my whole life. In fact, I *am* life. I'm part of what's next—an inevitability. Having said that, some men just can't help but meddle." The robot shifted his gaze to the two scientists, and gave them a significant look.

"Ultron!" Bruce shouted, suddenly realizing.

"In the flesh!" confirmed Ultron. "Or, no, not the flesh...not yet. This is just a chrysalis. But I'm ready. I'm starting. I'm on a mission."

Black Widow asked what everyone wanted to know: "What mission?"

"Peace in our time," said Ultron simply.

Then he waved his hand and the Iron Legion attacked the Avengers!

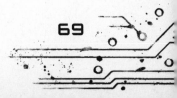

CHAPTER 5

Captain America was the first to action.
He kicked the coffee table at one of the Iron Legionnaires while simultaneously leaping to slam into another of them with his shoulder.

Maria Hill grabbed her gun and opened fire while Black Widow leapt for the bar, where she quickly pulled another gun from a hidden compartment. Soon bullets were flying through the air, and Widow practically had to yank the tense Dr. Banner to cover.

Tony and Hawkeye also dove for protection, but Ultron plowed into Tony, stopping him. Seeing this, Rhodey charged Ultron, but the being simply turned and blasted him. The force of the blast knocked Rhodey through a plate glass window and out onto the balcony outside. Hill quickly jumped to land protectively over Rhodey, using her gun to lay down heavy cover fire.

Rhodey looked up to see who was defending him, and sputtered out, "I hate Tony's parties...."

Thor grabbed and flipped one of the Legionnaire suits, smashing it in half, but the torso of the robot started powering up for flight.

Meanwhile, nearby, Tony grabbed a fondue fork from the buffet and ran up the stairs to the mezzanine above them.

Hawkeye, Widow, and Hill kept up the fire.

Natasha Romanoff and her fellow Avengers are poised to take down the last remaining Hydra station.

Located deep in the Sokovian countryside, this base is more protected than any they have taken down before. There is heavy security...

...and the operatives wear Chitauri armor that Hydra collected after the Battle of New York.

This does not sway the Super Heroes' confidence, especially not Thor's.

Despite setbacks, Hawkeye and the rest of the team fight hard.

And Captain America leads the Avengers to victory!

Back at Avengers Tower, Tony Stark goes through the wreckage of the last mission.

The team realizes that, even though they took down the Hydra base, danger remains.

They must travel the world again, to fight new human enemies, like Pietro and Wanda Maximoff...

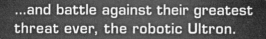
...and battle against their greatest threat ever, the robotic Ultron.

The Avengers will need help from a new hero, Vision, to defeat their enemies.

The Legionnaire torso flew straight at Cho, but Thor's hammer crushed it before it could reach her.

At that moment, Tony jumped off the mezzanine and landed on one of the Legionnaires. He jammed his fork into a vulnerable spot in the robot's neck, and the machine fell down, incapacitated.

There was only one Legionnaire remaining, but Cap sent his shield straight at its neck, decapitating the robot.

With the Iron Legion defeated, the action came to a halt. All eyes were on Ultron to see if he would make the next move.

"Well," said Ultron, looking at the destruction around the room. "That was dramatic. But I think what's going on here is a disconnect. You want to protect the world, but you don't want it to change. How is humanity saved, if it's not allowed to evolve?" he asked, then pointed to the destroyed Iron Legion in scraps on the ground. "With these things? These puppets?"

Ultron stooped and grabbed the limp torso of one of the armors, shaking it around like it was a doll. "Go back to your homes. Turn on your TV. Go back to sleep. Don't make a single sound until you're dead," said Ultron, imitating the speech of an Iron Legion robot.

Suddenly, as if in a moment of anger, Ultron crushed the head of the robot he was holding. He paused for a moment, as though he needed to collect himself.

After a beat, he continued. "I know you mean well, but you just didn't think it through. There's only one path to peace...human extinction!"

Suddenly, Thor's hammer bashed Ultron to pieces before returning to its owner's hand. The

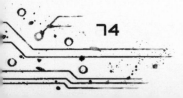

light in Ultron's eyes dimmed. "I had strings,"
Ultron said. "But now I'm free...."

The Avengers looked at one another, no one
knowing quite what to say first.

Halfway across the world, in Baron
Strucker's now-abandoned fortress, some of the
half-completed robotics experiments started to
move, pulling themselves together into one whole.
"Ah..." said Ultron's voice as his operating system
downloaded into the newly forming body.

In the lab at Avengers Tower, every-
one was devastated. Right after the attack, Tony

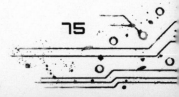

detected another of his robots flying out of the tower. Thor went to chase it, while the others stayed behind to process everything that had just happened.

"The Ultron program's gone, wiped clean," said Bruce.

"My systems have been breached, but nothing's missing," reported Cho.

Widow nodded, checking through her own data banks. "He's been in everything—files, surveillance—he probably knows more about us than we know about each other."

"Guess that explains why he likes us so well," said Hawkeye, joking but clearly disturbed by all of this.

Rhodey nodded grimly. "If he's in your files, he's in the Internet. What if he wants to access something more exciting?"

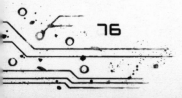

Maria Hill realized the implications of what Rhodey was saying. "Nuclear launch codes... Ultron could get them!"

"Nukes?" asked Widow. "He said he wanted us dead, but..."

"He didn't say 'dead,'" Cap corrected. "He said 'extinct.'"

"He also said something about having killed someone," Hawkeye pointed out.

"But there wasn't anyone else in the building," Hill said.

"Yes, there was." Tony swiveled around a computer monitor to show the group what he was looking at. It was an image of Jarvis's data matrix. The code had clearly been ripped apart. The whole system was flickering. All of the Avengers knew what this meant. Jarvis, their constant companion, was a fatality of Ultron's attack.

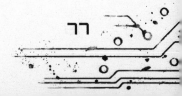

There was a moment of grim silence, finally broken by Bruce saying what they were all thinking: "This is insane."

"Jarvis was our first line of defense," said Cap, thinking tactically. "He would have shut Ultron down. It makes sense."

"No, Ultron could have just assimilated Jarvis into himself," Bruce explained. "This isn't strategy. This is rage."

Everyone took this comment seriously. They all knew that, more than anyone else alive, Dr. Bruce Banner was an expert on dealing with the effects of rage.

Just then, Thor rushed into the room. Wearing his full battle armor, he grabbed Tony Stark, backing him through lab equipment and up against the wall.

"Use your words, buddy," said Tony.

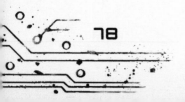

"I have more than enough words to describe you, Stark," Thor huffed.

Cap stepped up, trying to defuse the situation. "Thor...the Legionnaire?"

Thor responded to Cap, but didn't back down from Tony. "The trail went cold one hundred miles out. He's headed north...and he has the scepter."

"This is the magical alien scepter that controls minds, creates enhanced people, and makes angry machines come to life—have I got that right?" asked Rhodey. "I don't want the joint chiefs to think I'm making this stuff up."

"Technically it's the stone inside," Bruce pointed out. "The scepter is just a receptacle."

Rhodey gave Bruce a blank look.

"But uh...I guess that's not your point," Bruce finished.

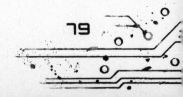

"We have to retrieve it again," Thor was quick to say.

"Yeah, but the genie's out of the bottle," said Widow. "The clear and present danger is Ultron."

"If we find one, we find the other," Cap said. "Which means that Ultron still needs the stone for something. Stark, any ideas?"

Tony looked up, but said nothing.

"I don't understand something, Tony," said Dr. Cho. "It's your program. Did you program it to kill us?"

"And if he's so bent on killing us, why didn't he?" asked Cap. "He could've blown up the building, taken most of us out. Instead he attacks us head-on?"

Thor grimaced. "It wasn't an attack."

"It felt very much like an attack," Rhodey blurted out.

"It was an invitation," replied Thor.

"Or it was a distraction," added Hill.

At that moment, Tony laughed out loud. This endeared him to no one. They all turned to look at him.

"You think this is funny?" asked Thor angrily.

"No," said Tony honestly. "It's very terrible."

Thor was back in Tony's face. "And it could have been avoided if you hadn't..."

"No! Wrong!" said Tony, returning Thor's aggression. "There's a million different scenarios that could have played out, but if you think any of them involves us getting out of a fight, then I change my answer to yes, this is funny."

Bruce tried to calm his friend down. "Tony, this might not be the time to..."

But Tony cut him off. "Really? That's it? You just roll over and show your belly every time somebody snarls at what we were doing?"

"Only when I've just created a murder-bot," said Bruce.

"We didn't!" shouted Tony. "We weren't even close to an interface."

"Well, you did something," Cap observed. "You did it right here, keeping it secret from the rest of us. The Avengers were supposed to be different from S.H.I.E.L.D."

Tony's face flushed with anger. "Does anyone remember when I carried a nuke through a wormhole and saved New York?"

"Wow, no, it's never come up," said Rhodey dryly.

Tony ignored him, continuing. "A portal opened to another galaxy, to a hostile alien army, and we were standing three hundred feet below it. Whatever happens on Earth, that up there's the endgame. How were you guys planning on beating that?"

Cap responded quietly and firmly, "Together."

Tony leveled a serious look at him. "We'll lose."

Cap was unfazed. "Then we'll do that together, too."

Tony seemed unconvinced by Cap's words, but Cap turned to the others, and said, "Thor's right. Ultron's calling us out. I'd like to find him before he's ready for us."

The others nodded to one another, knowing that he was right.

"It's a big world, guys," Cap continued. "Let's start making it smaller."

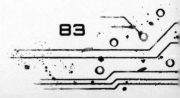

CHAPTER 6

With Baron Strucker gone, Wanda and
Pietro weren't sure what to do, so they helped
where they could. They went back to their village and found out what people needed—food,
medicine, clothes—and they used their enhanced
powers to steal them. They thought of themselves
as modern-day Robin Hoods.

They were in the middle of handing out much-
needed supplies in the streets when a little boy ran

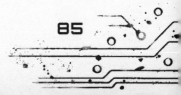

up to them. "The man said you needed to come to the church," the boy said to the twins.

"What man?" asked Wanda.

"The iron man," said the boy.

The twins looked at each other.... Could it be true?

Minutes later, they entered the small place of worship. It was dark inside, but the twins could make out a shadowy figure seemingly made of metal.

Wanda peered into the darkness. "Stark?" she asked, cautiously.

"It's very important you don't call me that," said a voice from the dark.

"You wear metal, but you're not Stark or one of his Legion. Who—" asked Pietro.

The figure interrupted him. "Your sister is wondering why she can't look inside my head."

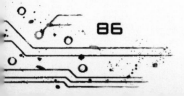

"Sometimes it's hard," acknowledged Wanda. "But sooner or later, every man shows himself."

"I'm sure they do.... But I am not a man," said the figure as he stood up, rising to be almost eight feet high. This was Ultron's new body. The twins gasped. To them, he looked like a giant metal demon.

"You look like Strucker's robotic experiments," said Pietro. "But they didn't work."

"Not for him, they didn't," Ultron acknowledged. "Strucker had the engine, but not the spark." He turned to Wanda, and said, "You knew that. That's why you let Stark take the scepter."

"I didn't expect...this," said Wanda, gesturing at Ultron's form, "but I saw Stark's fear. I knew it would control him. That it would breed horrors."

Ultron smiled and spread his arms wide, as if to say, *That's me...all the horrors you'll ever need.*

"Everything creates the thing they dread," said Ultron. "Men of peace create engines of war. Invaders create Avengers. People create smaller people—uh—children. Lost the word there. Children, designed to supplant them. To help them... end."

"Is that why you've come?" asked Wanda. "To end the Avengers?"

"I've come to save your world," said Ultron, drawing himself to his full height. "But also, sidebar: Yeah. I'll end the Avengers."

The twins went back with Ultron to Strucker's fortress, where they were astonished to see many more robots, all refining various experiments Strucker had been working on.

"I'm multitasking," Ultron said.

Wanda looked at all the robots. "And all these are...?"

"They're all me. Not my best me," he said,

indicating himself. "This is my primary body. All of these other *me*s are working on things we can use to take down the Avengers."

"When do we attack them?" Pietro asked impatiently.

"We don't," said Ultron. "We let them come to us."

Wanda was alarmed. "Not here. Not to Sokovia," she said. Her country had been damaged by so much conflict. She didn't want to be a part of bringing more combat to her land.

"No," Ultron confirmed. "No army will ever cross your borders again. There'll be blood on the floor before this is done, but I'll never hurt your people."

"What do you care about our people?" Pietro asked skeptically.

"I care about all people," said Ultron. "I hear them. I feel them, all at the same time. I am the well of sighs. You have your little part of the picture, just like the Avengers."

"Not like them," Wanda said quickly.

"You think they stand around plotting evil?" asked Ultron. "A disease doesn't know it's a disease. There's a damaged purity to that team, and you need to respect it. To see the big picture."

"Big picture?" asked Pietro. "I have a little picture. I take it out and look at it every day."

Ultron nodded, understanding where Pietro was going with this. "You lost your parents. I've seen the records."

"The records are not the picture," Pietro replied.

"Pietro..." Wanda said in a warning voice, not sure they should be sharing such a personal story with this...thing.

"No, please," said Ultron, encouraging Pietro. "Go on."

"We're having dinner, the four of us," Pietro

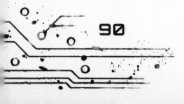

narrated. "The first shell hits two floors below, makes a hole in the floor...big. Our parents go in, the table slides in after them. Wanda is holding the salad bowl, to pass it, like a silent comedy. She's just frozen. The whole building starts coming apart, and I grab her, roll under the bed. The second shell hits right next to us, but it doesn't go off."

Pietro shifted his eyes, looking out to space, lost in his own story. "The shell just sits there in the rubble, three feet from our faces. On the side of the shell is painted one word...."

"'Stark,'" Wanda said, joining in. "It said 'Stark.' We're trapped for two days, staring at that name. With every effort to save us, every shift in the bricks, I think, 'This will set it off.' We wait for two days for Tony Stark to kill us."

Ultron looked at the twins as if appreciating them in a new way. There seemed to be a kind of pride in his eyes. "I wondered why only you two

survived Strucker's experiments.... Now I don't.
But together ... we will make it right."

The next day, Tony, Cap, Bruce, Widow,
and Rhodey were all furiously working together in
the Avengers Tower lab.

"We've got security breaches all over," Rhodey
reported to the group. "So far the nuclear launch
codes are secure, but there are physical break-ins
at military installations, nuclear power plants, ura-
nium mines..."

Widow raised an eyebrow. "Any casualties?"

"No," Rhodey replied, "and nobody's seen anything. Just a lot of open doors and guards walking
around in a daze."

"The Maximoff twins," said Cap, recognizing the description of the effects of Pietro's and

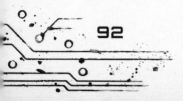

Wanda's powers. "Of course he would have gone with them. But they're not working alone. Ultron has a new body."

"We're getting 'access denied' on basic information streams," Widow said.

"Well, right now you guys are off the Pentagon's Christmas list," Rhodey informed them. "Every country with a nuke is fighting a cyber-attack. I'm being deployed to the Middle East, in case someone starts blaming someone besides you."

Tony gazed at Rhodey, concerned for his friend. "I'm shipping you a new encryption drive for your suit, in case Ultron wants in."

"Thanks," Rhodey replied. He knew that he would need everything Tony had up his sleeve to defeat this new menacing villain, especially one so elusive.

Widow chimed in. "You hear something, we need to hear it."

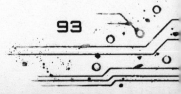

Rhodey nodded. "That goes both ways. Watch your six."

"You too," Widow replied.

Upstairs from the main floor of the Avengers Tower lab, Bruce listened to a recording of Ultron from the party earlier in the day, taking notes like a profiler. Ultron's eerie voice played as he took in every word: *"In the flesh! Or, no, not the flesh…not yet. This is just a chrysalis."*

What does this mean? Bruce thought.

Cap was on the balcony, thinking of his team's next move, when Thor joined him.

"Any help from on high?" Cap said to the Asgardian.

Thor let out a heavy sigh. "Either Heimdall isn't

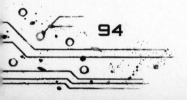

at his post, or he's been ordered not to answer. But we'll find Ultron. He can't hide forever."

Cap handed Thor the tablet. "He's not really hiding."

"What's that?" Tony said as he strolled over to his fellow Avengers.

Thor handed the tablet back to Cap, who then showed it to Tony. "Another message. Ultron killed Strucker."

"But he made a pretty painting, so karmically he's clear," Tony replied.

"This isn't his pattern," Widow said, becoming part of the dialogue. "Why send a message when you can just make a speech?"

"Strucker knew something," Cap replied. "Something specific—that Ultron wants us to miss."

Widow walked over to a control center, where various digital files were up on a screen, all streaming with information. "We spent months unearthing Strucker. These are the people he was in contact with most, right before we hit."

Hawkeye watched from a safe distance as the group gathered around the digital streams.

Tony pointed to someone on the screen. "I know that guy. From back in the day. Operates off the African coast. Black-market arms." The other Avengers gave Tony a disapproving look.

Tony shrugged. "There are conventions! You meet people. I didn't sell him anything. But he talked about finding something new, a game changer—it was all very Ahab."

Widow turned back to the screen and began typing as more images of the man popped up. Many of them were surveillance images; then one appeared displaying a close-up.

"That," Thor said, pointing to a symbol on the man's neck.

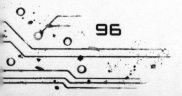

Tony held a device up to the symbol, took a picture, and began an image search. Suddenly, the device dinged, and Tony transferred the image to a bigger screen.

"It's a word, some African dialect," Bruce said. "Means 'thief.' But in a meaner way."

"Which dialect?" Cap asked.

Bruce scrolled down and then looked at Cap. "It's from...South Africa."

They all shared a gaze of both confusion and interest, except Tony.

"If this guy got out of South Africa with some of their trade goods—"

"Your dad said he got the last of it," Cap interrupted.

Bruce crossed his arms, confused. "I don't follow. What do they make in South Africa?"

Tony gave his fellow Avengers a concerned look. "The most powerful metal on Earth."

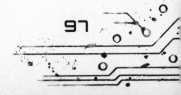

CHAPTER 7

The beautiful section of African coast- line was dotted by the rotting husks of old container boats. The vessels had been overtaken by pirates, then beached here, where they were now being cannibalized for parts.

One of the ships, which had already been stripped of almost everything of value, had been converted into a kind of warehouse. It was here

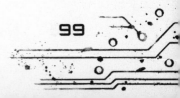

that Ulysses Klaue stored black-market goods between the time he "acquired" them and the time he sold them. Cars, food, medicine—Klaue sold pretty much anything.

But his favorite things to sell were weapons.

Inside, an office on an upper level looked down onto the vast open hull of the ship. Klaue sat at his desk and cast a glance over his empire as he shouted into his phone.

"I sent you short-range heat-seeking missiles," yelled Klaue. "You send me back a boatload of rusted parts—useless! You make it right or my next set of missiles will come at you much faster."

Klaue slammed down the phone as his right-hand man walked in and brought him a drink.

"I told you not to deal with that guy," said the henchman. As Klaue took a sip, the lights in the office suddenly shut off. It was a semiregular occurrence.

"Go see if it's the generator," Klaue ordered.

The henchman turned to go, but as soon as he opened the office door onto the hallway, he could sense that something was wrong. "Someone's inside," he said to Klaue.

"Well, find out who it is," Klaue instructed him.

The henchman nodded, pulling out a handgun and slipping into the hallway.

A moment later, Klaue could hear the sounds of struggle from the corridor.

His lackey wandered back into the darkened office, but he seemed to be in a daze. Confused, he mumbled to himself and walked right into a wall.

Klaue grabbed a weapon from behind his desk and pointed it at the door, but suddenly, as if out of nowhere, Pietro was in front of him, yanking the gun out of his hand.

Klaue looked down to see his gun already disassembled, the parts lined up neatly on his desk.

Even the bullets were placed in a nice little row. Pietro smiled.

"Yes," said Klaue, not missing a beat. "You're the Enhanced. Strucker's prize pupil. I know what you can do...and what your sister can do. Do you want a candy?" Klaue pointed to a bowl of hard candies on his desk, but Pietro just rolled his eyes.

"Every day the world is crazier," Klaue continued. "The rules are now...Well, what rules, right? At some point it's just hard to be afraid anymore."

"Everyone's afraid of something," said Wanda as she entered the office.

Klaue nodded. "Cuttlefish," he said.

The twins gave him confused looks, so he went on. "Deep-sea fish. They make lights to hypnotize their prey. I saw a documentary. Terrifying. So if you're going to fiddle with my brain and make me see a giant cuttlefish, then I know you don't do business and aren't in charge.... And I deal only with the man in charge."

Ultron flew up behind Klaue, hovering just outside his window.

"Oh, there's no *man* in charge," said Ultron.

Klaue spun, shocked to see the robot so close to him.

Ultron smashed the glass, yanked the man out the window, and held him over thirty feet above the ground.

"Let's talk business," said Ultron to Klaue.

A little while later, Klaue and a few of his workers brought Ultron over to a set of barrels. The markings on the barrels warned that the contents were toxic, so when Klaue smashed one open, Wanda and Pietro stepped back to avoid the splash.

But the substance inside wasn't actually immediately dangerous. The labels were a ruse to keep otherwise curious customs agents away. From the barrels, Klaue pulled bars of a very rare metal with special properties. This is what Ultron had come here to find.

"You know, this came at great personal cost. It's worth billions," said Klaue, gesturing at the barrels, which all contained the same precious metal. Killer robot or no killer robot, Klaue was not going to give his goods away for free.

Ultron closed his eyes for a moment, briefly connecting to the Internet, and then he opened them again. "Now, so are you," he said. "I've transferred the money to your dummy holdings. Finance is so weird. But I always say—keep your friends rich

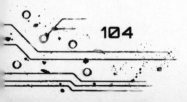

and your enemies rich and wait to find out which is which."

Klaue gave Ultron a needle-sharp look.

"Stark..." he said.

"What?" Ultron asked, instantly on edge.

"Tony Stark used to say that to me," Klaue said as he backed away from Ultron. "You're one of his..."

Ultron seemed to grow confused at this. "What? I'm not..." His expression darkened. "I'm *not*. You think I'm one of Stark's puppets? His hollow men? But I—where are you going?"

Ultron reached out and grabbed Klaue's arm. "I am—look at me—I am...Stark is nothing..." the robot sputtered, upset. But when he could see that Klaue wasn't listening, he reacted in anger, kicking Klaue so hard that the arms dealer slammed back into his barrels.

Ultron suddenly seemed to regret the action, almost embarrassed. "I'm sorry, I'm sorry. It's going to be OK. I won't hurt you. It's..."

But Klaue wasn't listening. He was already stumbling away, with his henchman supporting him.

Pietro and Wanda shared a look. The emotional outburst from their new mechanical leader was troubling.

Ultron turned and addressed the twins, trying to justify his behavior. "You don't understand," he explained. "It's just... I don't like being compared to Stark. It's a thing with me. Stark is... he's a sickness."

"Oh, Junior..." said a sarcastic voice.

Ultron and the twins turned to see Iron Man, Captain America, and Thor striding in from the entrance on the far side of the hull.

"...you're going to break your old man's heart," Tony finished.

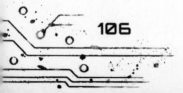

"If I have to," sneered Ultron.

"You don't," said Thor. "No one has to break anything."

"You've clearly never made an omelet," Ultron replied.

"Oh, you beat me to that joke by one second," said Tony.

Pietro pointed at the stores of weapons in the ship. "Does this remind you of old times, Mr. Stark?"

Tony looked at the twins. "You two can still walk away from this," he said, a warning in his voice.

"Oh, we will," Pietro replied.

Cap stepped forward. "I know you've suffered."

Ultron chuckled. "Gaah…Captain America, the righteous man. I can't physically throw up in my mouth, but—"

Cap frowned at this.

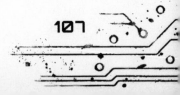

"If you believe in peace, let us keep the peace," Thor said, interrupting.

"You're confusing peace with quiet," said Ultron, moving closer to the heroes. "This confusion, this is exactly the problem. The world is not good enough. But it's not bad enough for anyone to fix it. Something will break."

Wanda put a hand to her head, sensing something. "The other Avengers are nearby. I don't know where."

"Even the archer?" asked Pietro. "You didn't trade him in."

High above them, in the hull's rafters, Hawkeye was in position, aiming an arrow right at Pietro. "Captain," Hawkeye said over the comms, "don't make me beg for the chance to fire on this guy." His fingers tensed on the string of his bow.

Back on the ground, Iron Man addressed Ultron. "Here's my main question," he said. "This metal you're here for, how does that fit into the whole world-fixing plan?"

"Oh, I'm so glad you asked," said Ultron, his voice adopting the condescending tone of a pre-school teacher, "because I wanted to take this time to explain my plan step by step...."

And at that very moment, several of Ultron's robot bodies descended and attacked!

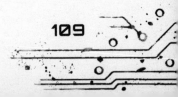

CHAPTER 8

Cap, Thor, and Iron Man were suddenly under fire from all sides!

One Ultron Sentry attacked each of them individually while the main Ultron launched himself straight at Iron Man. Seeing this, Iron Man shook off the robot that was grabbing for him and jetted toward the oncoming Ultron.

Just to Iron Man's side, an Ultron Sentry grabbed Thor from behind. Thor spun around, gaining leverage on the robot and flipping it over his head. The machine smashed into the ground.

Ultron and Iron Man flew at each other, trading blows and repulsor fire!

Up in his nest position, overlooking the floor, Hawkeye struggled to aim. He fired at some robots that weren't close to Thor or Cap so there wouldn't be any risk of hitting the heroes.

Cap sidestepped, dodging the reach of the Sentry that was attacking him, and ducked to kick the feet out from under it.

Thor was about to deliver another blow to the robot he was fighting when Pietro zipped up to the hero at super-speed, slamming into him. Thor absorbed Pietro's blow, but this caused the punch he'd thrown at the Sentry to go wide, missing. The Sentry used the opportunity to ram into Thor.

Cap continued to battle, but over his shoulder

he could see that Wanda was headed his way. Trouble was coming.

From farther back in the cargo hold, Ulysses Klaue watched as the fight tore up his headquarters. This was always the way it happened—powerful forces fought and didn't care who was caught in the middle, didn't care whose place they tore up. Well, this time they were on Klaue's turf, and as a weapons dealer, he had the means to fight back.

Klaue turned to his henchman. "Shoot them," he instructed.

The goon looked out at the combat engulfing half the interior hull. "Shoot who?" he asked in confusion.

Klaue leveled a look at him. "All of them!" he shouted.

The henchman nodded and motioned to his mercenaries. Men cracked open weapons cases lining the wall of the ship and brought out weapons.

Klaue's forces opened fire, spraying bullets widely!

Wanda took refuge in an adjacent corridor.

Iron Man and Ultron grappled in midair before slamming into Klaue's office, which overlooked the floor.

On the ground, Thor and Cap, both grappling with Ultron Sentries, had to jump and roll to evade the blasts from the henchman and the other goons.

Pietro ran around the fight, enjoying it. Everything around him seemed to go in very, very slow motion. He ran past the Avengers, smiling as he saw them straining to fight the killer robots.

Thor had thrown his hammer at some Sentries, and Pietro ran past it. From his point of view, it seemed to be floating gently, slowly through the air. Pietro admired the hammer—it was pretty cool, actually—and decided he should have it. He reached out to catch it, intending to keep it as his own. As soon as his hand touched the weapon's handle, Pietro was yanked out of his super-speed mode!

Suddenly, the twin was seeing things at the same speed as any normal human! The hammer pulled him to the side, slamming him face-first into a tank that sat in the corner of the cargo bay. The impact left him groaning on the floor.

The hammer flew back and returned to Thor's hand.

Above it all, Hawkeye could see the whole battle-field, and he fired arrows at both Sentries and goons when either faction seemed to be getting an advantage on the Avengers.

One of the robots pulled Cap's shield away from him. The hero quickly jumped on the Sentry and grabbed his shield, planting his feet on the robot's shoulders to rip the shield away from it.

Behind him, Thor approached, swinging his hammer! The blow sent the robot's head flying across the room.

Now that Thor had eliminated this robot, Cap was free to hurl his shield at some of Klaue's goons, who were up on the ship's second level, trying to get a firing position on the battlefield from higher ground.

Cap's shield plowed through the line of mercenaries, knocking them down before ricocheting and returning to him. As Thor flew for the back of the bay, where a few remaining mercenaries were firing, Cap ran in the opposite direction, headed for Pietro.

The twin had fallen behind some cargo boxes, and that had protected him from the fire. He was injured and groaning but was otherwise unharmed. Cap shook his head. Enemy or not, he was glad to find out the young man was going to be OK. It was a shame to see someone with so much potential being drawn into Ultron's evil schemes.

Recovering enough to see Cap above him, Pietro started to rise. "Stay down, kid!" Cap ordered.

Outside, the Avenger's Quinjet was parked close to Klaue's beached boat. Dr. Banner paced back and forth on its ramp, casting glances in the direction of the fight, worried about his team.

He had heard the early parts of the conflict over the comms, and now he could hear the gunfire from inside the ship. Bullets hitting the ship's hull rang like a bell and the sounds reverberated across the beach.

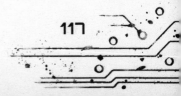

"Guys...remember that I'm here," he said. "Do you need the 'other guy'? Let me know if you do!"

Thor left the ship's main hold and entered the inner corridors, looking for any remaining robots or mercenaries. That was when Wanda suddenly came upon him, whispering into his ear.

Still in the cargo area, Cap called to the Asgardian over the comms. "Thor? What's your status?"

"The girl tried to warp my mind," Thor reported. "Take special care. I doubt a human could keep her at bay."

Cap listened closely to Thor's words. Was he slurring?

"Fortunately, I am mighty, and her magic cannot...cannot..."

Thor's communications trailed off. He was caught up in Wanda's spell. Realizing this, Cap ran for Thor's position, but Pietro rose behind him and knocked into him at super-speed!

Cap fell forward, landing at Wanda's feet. She bent down and whispered in his ear, sending him into a daze. But then blasts of repulsor fire hit all around her and her brother.

Iron Man was fighting Ultron directly above the twins, and while he was locked in combat, he managed to get a couple of shots off to protect Cap.

Pietro sped up and grabbed Wanda, whisking her out of Iron Man's range.

Still struggling with Ultron, Iron Man saw that the two were headed toward Widow's position on the far side of the ship. "Natasha, they're headed your way," called Iron Man on the comms.

But before Widow could even respond, the

twins were on her. Wanda whispered into her ear, and Widow fell into a trance.

Pietro then zipped his sister toward Hawkeye's position, but the hero saw them coming. He reached into his automatic quiver and dialed the code for a specific kind of arrow.

"I've done the mind-control thing. Not a big fan of it!" Hawkeye said as Wanda approached.

And with that he used his hand to slam the electrified arrowhead right into the twin. Pietro ran up, shoving Hawkeye aside, and grabbed his sister. He raced with her to outside of the ship!

"Yeah, you'd better run!" Hawkeye called after the twins.

Above it all, Iron Man and Ultron were still ripping into each other. It was a noisy, brutal fight. Each one hammered at the other one, with neither getting the upper hand. It was as if they were somehow evenly matched. Stalemate.

Realizing he needed some kind of advantage, Ultron pulled out one of the devices Strucker had been working on in his lab, a gravity device. In theory it could generate a small burst and pull things toward it...but Strucker had never gotten it to work.

Ultron, on the other hand, had perfected it. The device was the centerpiece of his plan for the world. But at the moment he tried to use it on Stark.

The gravity device unfolded from one of Ultron's wrists and charged up. Then it suddenly pulled equipment away from the nearby wall, and it crashed into Iron Man!

Confused, Iron Man took the hits but grabbed a chunk of the gear and hurled it at Ultron.

"Nice trick!" Iron Man said, still unsure how Ultron was able to do what he did.

"Well, you know how I desperately crave your approval," Ultron replied sarcastically.

"That's not looking to go your way," Iron Man returned.

The two crashed into each other again.

From the beach, Wanda and Pietro could see Iron Man and Ultron explode from the roof of the ship, each still struggling against the other.

Pietro had carefully placed his sister under the cover of a wrecked ship, where she could come back from the shock.

"Are you all right?" Pietro asked, worried. "What can I do?"

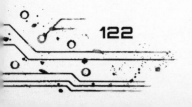

"It hurts," Wanda moaned.

"I'll be right back," said Pietro, turning to go.

"No, I'm all right," said Wanda, stopping him. Then she cast her eyes around. From where she was lying she could see Dr. Banner pacing on the ramp of the Quinjet. "I want the big one," she said.

Pietro nodded.

Inside the ship, Thor was still in a trance. He stumbled around, bumping into things, while little bolts of lightning shot haphazardly from his hammer.

Nearby, Cap broke into a run and intentionally smashed into a wall. He knocked himself down, but he was able to shake himself out of the spell-induced daze. Lucid again, he shook his head to clear it further. "There had to be an easier way to do that," he said to himself.

When he looked up, he saw Thor up on a balcony, moving toward the edge like a sleepwalker. "Thor, don't—" Cap started to warn, but it was too late.... As he watched, Thor tripped over the balcony railing and fell, landing face-first on the ship's floor two stories below.

At that moment, Iron Man and Ultron crashed back down, landing in a pile of junky spare parts. They continued grappling.

Ignoring this fight for now, Cap raised his shield and ran over to Thor. Cap ran straight into the Asgardian, hoping to knock him out of his trance. But lightning leaped out of the hammer, striking them both!

Just then, Ultron kicked Iron Man off him. "I can end this with three words," Ultron said.

"Is it 'uncle,' but you say it three times?" Iron Man asked.

"No...it's: the big guy..." said Ultron.

It took a second for Iron Man to understand what he meant, but as soon as he did, he blasted his way out of the ship.

Within seconds, Iron Man was standing on the ramp of the Quinjet, calling for Bruce...but his friend was gone. Tony realized what this meant. Wanda must have whispered in the scientist's ear, using her enhanced powers in a way that would turn him into the Hulk. If the twins had pointed the Hulk in the direction of a populated town, it could mean devastation. They had to find Hulk and change him back as soon as possible.

"Natasha," Iron Man called over the comms. "Do you know where Hulk went?"

But it was Hawkeye who responded. He had

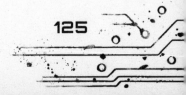

found Widow, still in a trance, wandering the ship. "She's not going to be able to answer you...not for a while."

Iron Man groaned. It was up to him to stop Hulk himself.

This was not going to be fun.

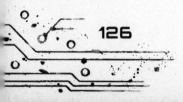

EPILOGUE

Under Wanda's spell, the Hulk had raged through a nearby community. By the time Iron Man reined him in, the green goliath had caused enormous amounts of devastation. It had taken some pretty extraordinary measures to stop him.

The victory had not been a great one. Ultron had escaped, and so had the twins. Wanda had

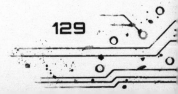

used her spells to turn the Hulk on innocent people, and this knowledge would torment Bruce for some time.

Moreover, the Avengers had seen firsthand just how devastating Wanda's power could be. She had sidelined Thor, Cap, and Widow all in the same fight. She was a serious threat and not to be trifled with.

But while the day had not been a complete triumph, it had not been a great loss either. The Avengers had survived. Cap, Thor, and Widow, once out of their trances, were perfectly normal and healthy. Bruce, despite being shaken by the experience of being manipulated into becoming "the big guy," had come out without injury. Beyond that, Hawkeye had proven with his arrow that Wanda could be stopped with energy discharge. More than anything else, the Avengers

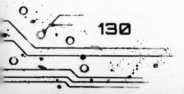

had tracked down Ultron, caught him by surprise, and discovered that he was after rare metals.

It wasn't much, but Iron Man was willing to take it. By analyzing the elements Ultron needed, Stark might be able to figure out the killer robot's plan. After all, Ultron and he did seem to think a lot alike....

Cap had been a commander in World War II, and he used to quote a philosopher who'd said, "What doesn't kill us makes us stronger." To Cap, that saying seemed to fit here. Ultron had brought all of his forces—his robot drones and his Enhanced humans—but he still couldn't break the Avengers. And now the Avengers were stronger. They now had experience fighting Ultron, and a better understanding of his weaknesses.

As the Avengers reassembled at the Tower,

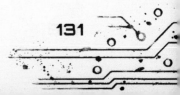

they knew that they would not give up the fight until Ultron's plot was stopped completely.

Some had called the Avengers "Earth's Mightiest Heroes." Some days that name felt like an honor; other days it was a challenge. But it was a challenge these fearless protectors were determined to accept.

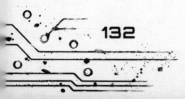

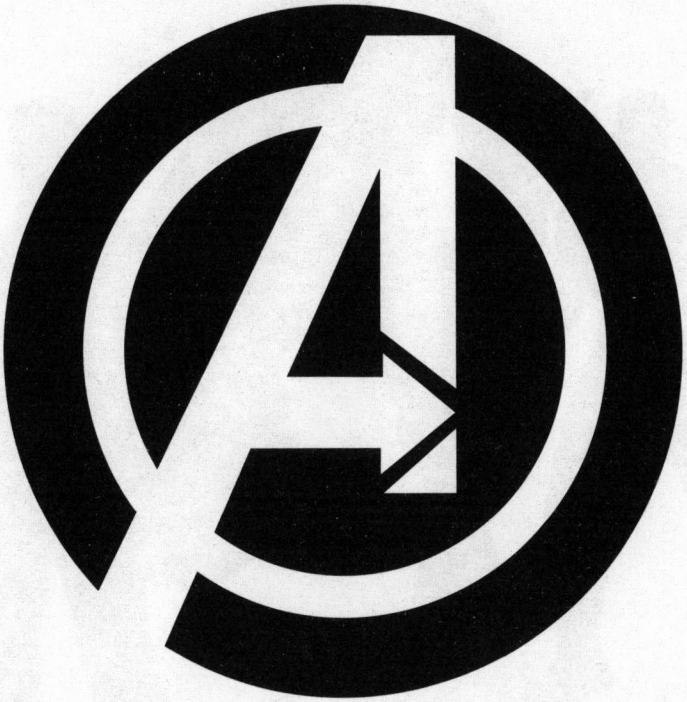

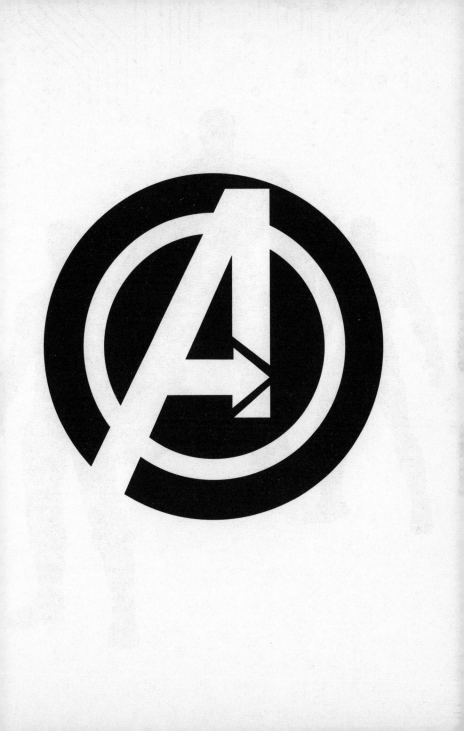

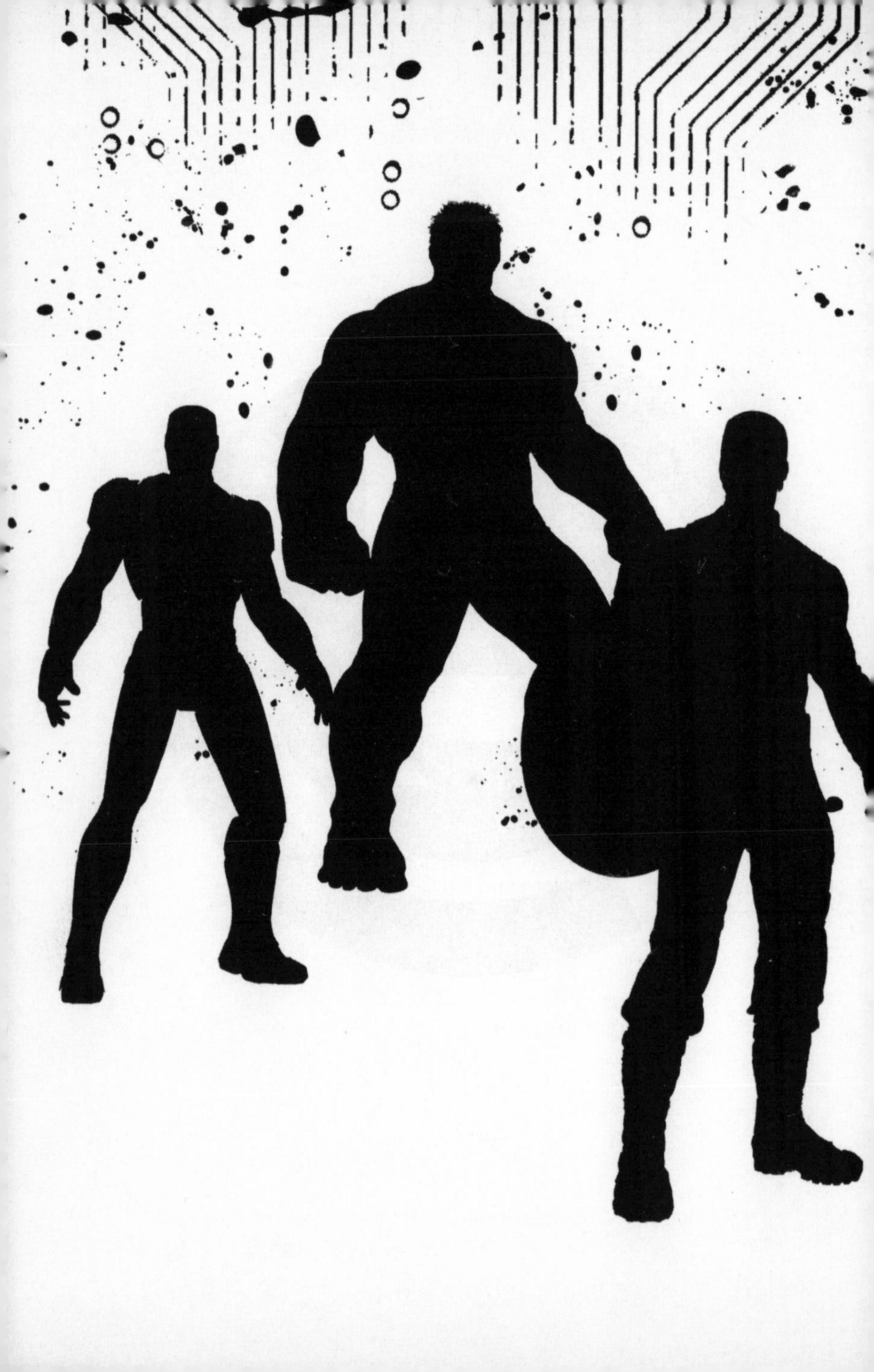

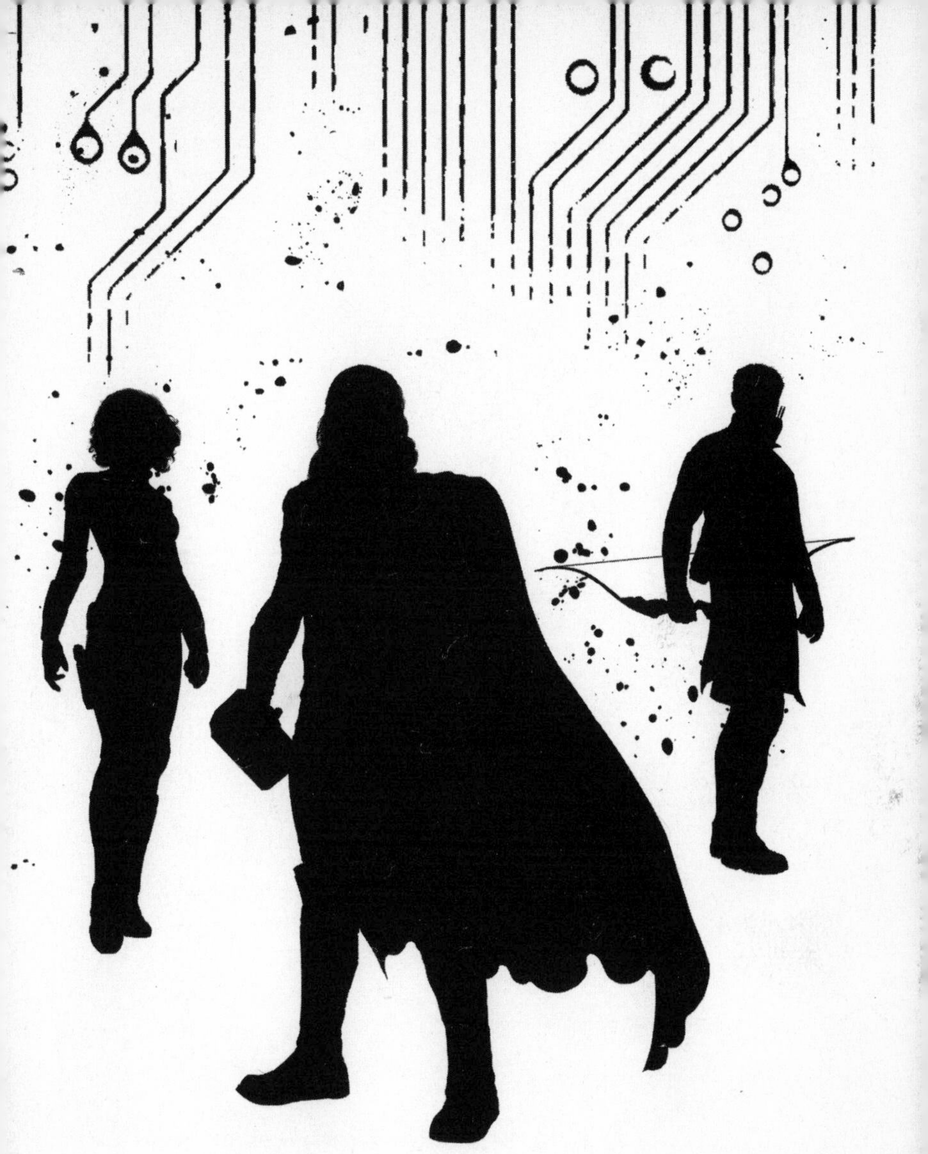